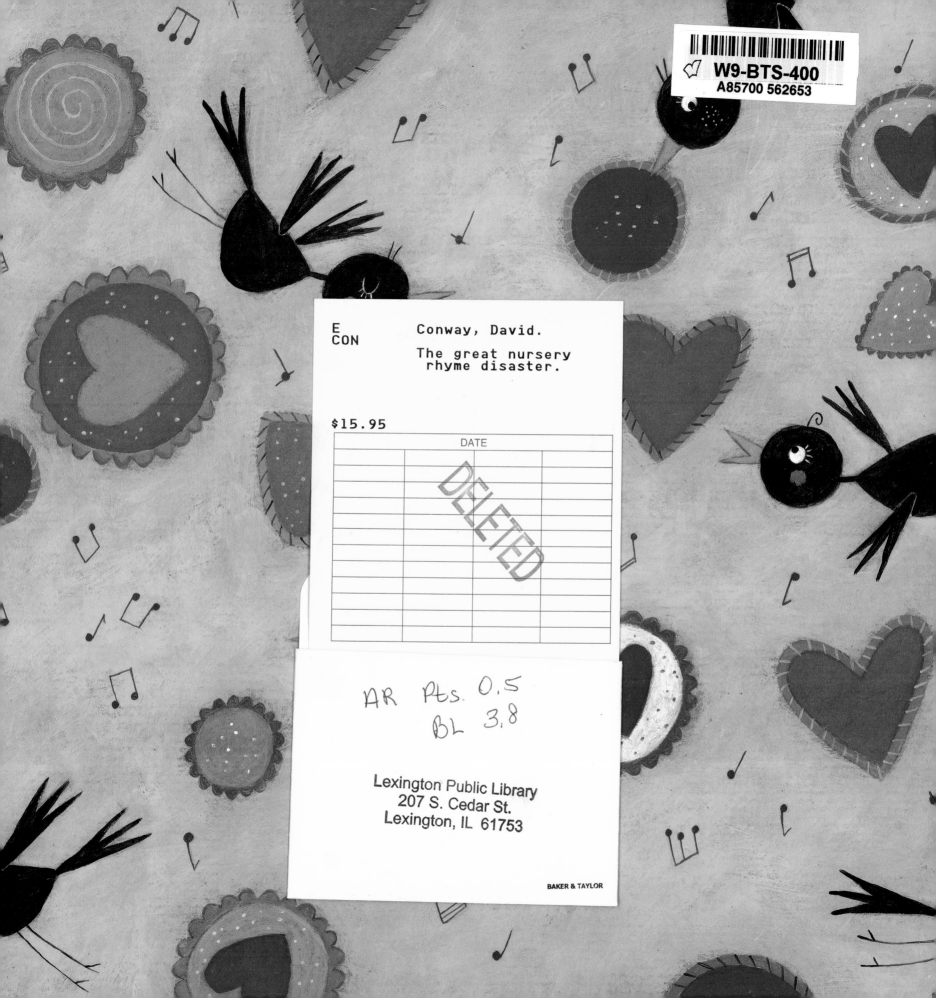

FOR BERNIE FOLAN, WITH ALL MY LOVE —*D.C.*

FOR GRAN AND AUNT NORA—YOU'D HAVE LOVED THIS! —*M.W.*

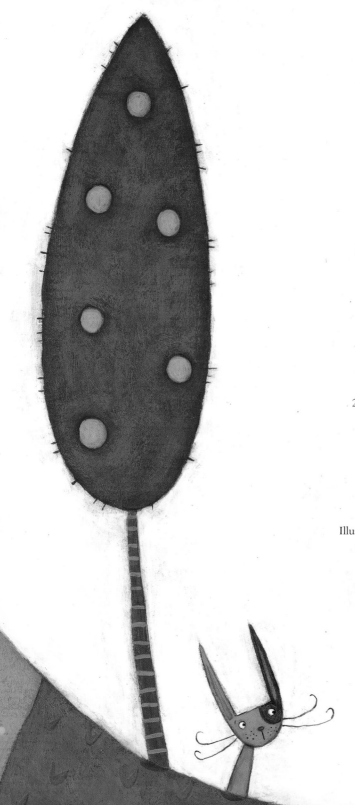

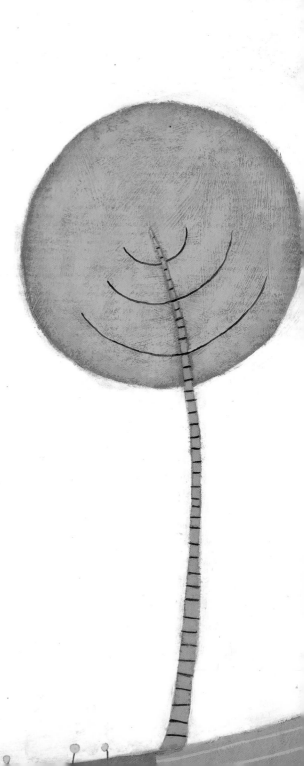

tiger tales

an imprint of ME Media, LLC

202 Old Ridgefield Road, Wilton, CT 06897

Published in the United States 2009

Originally published in Great Britain 2008

by Hodder Children's Books

a division of Hachette Children's Books

Text copyright ©2008 David Conway

Illustrations copyright ©2008 Melanie Williamson

CIP data is available

ISBN-13: 978-1-58925-080-2

ISBN-10: 1-58925-080-X

Printed in China

THE GREAT NURSERY RHYME DISASTER

BY

DAVID CONWAY

ILLUSTRATED BY
MELANIE WILLIAMSON

tiger tales

LITTLE MISS MUFFET WAS BORED.

She was bored of being in the same old nursery rhyme and she'd had quite enough of that scary, little spider.

"What I need," she told herself, "is a change."

So off she went into the pages of the book to find another nursery rhyme to be in.

First she met the grand old Duke of York.

"May I be in your rhyme?" Little Miss Muffet asked politely.

"Of course," said the Duke.

"GET IN LINE!"

Oh, the grand old Duke of York,
He had ten thousand men;
He marched them and Miss Muffet up
to the top of the hill,
And he marched them down again.

"Oh no!" cried Miss Muffet. "This rhyme has way too much marching for my taste."

And with that, she slipped away into the next pages of the book to find a better rhyme to be in.

NEXT RHYME

Soon after, she saw Jack and Jill going up a hill. They were happy to let Little Miss Muffet try out their rhyme....

JACK AND JILL AND MISS MUFFET
WENT UP THE HILL,
TO FETCH A PAIL OF WATER;
MISS MUFFET FELL DOWN
AND BROKE HER CROWN,
AND JACK AND JILL
CAME TUMBLING AFTER.

"This nursery rhyme is too painful," complained Little Miss Muffet, hobbling off to find a rhyme that didn't hurt so much.

On the next page, Little Miss Muffet spotted a mouse by an old grandfather clock.

"May I be in your rhyme?" she asked.

"Absolutely!" said the mouse. "I'm tired of running up and down that clock."

HICKORY, DICKORY, DOCK,
MISS MUFFET CLIMBED
UP THE CLOCK.
THE CLOCK STRUCK ONE,
MISS MUFFET SLID DOWN,
HICKORY, DICKORY, DOCK.

"I look ridiculous!"
said Little Miss Muffet,
as her cheeks turned almost
purple with embarrassment.

And she quickly sneaked
off to find a rhyme that
didn't make her look so silly.

NAUGHTY
BOYS

Further on, Little Miss Muffet met little Johnny Flynn and Tommy Stout. The two boys giggled to each other as they let her try out their rhyme. . . .

DING, DONG, BELL, MISS MUFFET'S IN THE WELL. WHO PUT HER IN? LITTLE JOHNNY FLYNN. WHO PULLED HER OUT? LITTLE TOMMY STOUT.

A very wet Miss Muffet **screamed** and ran into the next pages of the book as fast as she could to find a rhyme that had no mean boys in it!

JUMPING COW →

yummy candy

It wasn't long before Little Miss Muffet
ran into a dish and a spoon.

"May I be in your rhyme?" she asked.

"Yes, you can play the part of the dish,"
said the cow.

"Splendid!" said the cow. But the dish wasn't happy and a terrible ruckus broke out all over the page.

"I'LL HAVE YOU KNOW THAT I'VE BEEN RUNNING AWAY WITH THAT SPOON EVER SINCE THIS RHYME WAS WRITTEN!"

hollered the dish.

FOLLOW FOR
blackbird pies

The ruckus spilled over onto the next page…

The Queen of Hearts **wasn't** making tarts anymore, but Itsy Bitsy Spider was.

Mary **didn't** have a little lamb, but instead was followed by three blind mice.

And it **wasn't** Humpty Dumpty falling off the wall, but Old Mother Hubbard!

While all this was going on, Little Miss Muffet, who by now had decided that she no longer needed a change, tiptoed quietly back through the pages of the book and returned to her very own rhyme. . . .

But she soon remembered
why she had wanted a change
in the first place!

LITTLE MISS MUFFET SAT ON A TUFFET,
EATING HER CURDS AND WHEY;
ALONG CAME A SPIDER,
WHO SAT DOWN BESIDE HER
AND FRIGHTENED MISS MUFFET AWAY.

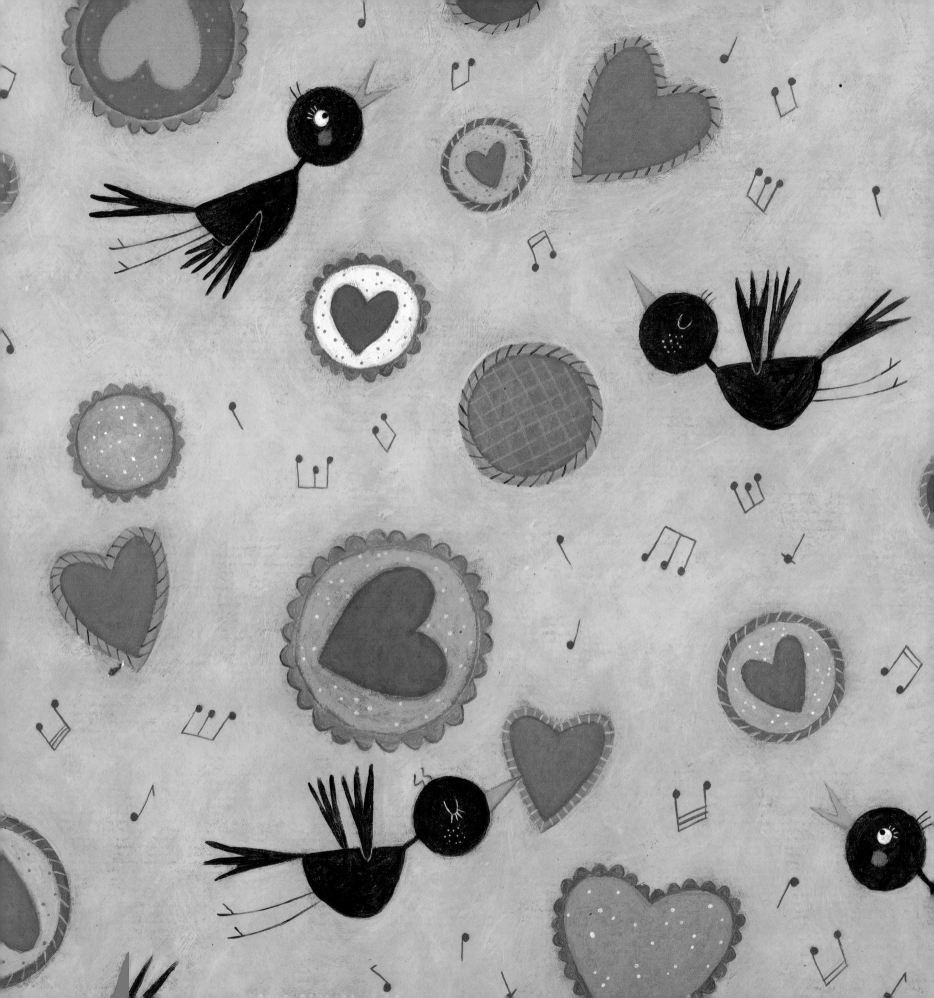